West Moon Street

by

ROB URBINATI

**Based on "Lord Arthur Savile's Crime"
by Oscar Wilde**

A SAMUEL FRENCH ACTING EDITION

SAMUEL FRENCH

FOUNDED 1830

NEW YORK HOLLYWOOD LONDON TORONTO

SAMUELFRENCH.COM

ISBN 978-0-573-65148-9   Printed in U.S.A.   #25280

MUSIC USE NOTE

IMPORTANT BILLING AND CREDIT
REQUIREMENTS

WEST MOON STREET was developed in a Playwrights Workshop at Doane College in Nebraska, as part of their Summer Research Program, under the supervision of Project Director Eric Selk.

WEST MOON STREET was originally produced by Prospect Theater Company (Cara Reichel, Producing Artistic Director / Melissa Huber, Managing Director) at the Hudson Guild Theatre, April 21 - May 20, 2007, under the direction of Davis McCallum with the following cast and production staff:

LORD ARTHUR SAVILE . . . . David Ruffin
LADY WINDERMERE. . . . . Judith Hawking
SYBIL MERTON . . . . Melissa Miller
CHARLES . . . . .Alex Webb
LADY CLEM. . . . . Glenn Peters
JANE PERCY . . . . .Jocelyn Greene
MR. PODGERS . . . . Avi Glickstein
HERR WINCKELKOPF . . . . Michael Crane
THE PIANIST . . . . William Demaniow

Quincy D. Morris, Stage Manager
Valerie Lentz, Assistant Stage Manager
Lee Savage, Set Designer
Naomi Wolff, Costume Designer
Lily Fossner, Lighting Designer
Russell M. Kaplan, Composer

CHARACTERS

LORD ARTHUR SAVILE, a gentleman
Naïve

LADY WINDERMERE, his confidante
Grand

SYBIL MERTON, his betrothed
Clever

CHARLES, his valet
Devoted

LADY CLEM, his elderly aunt
Irritable

JANE PERCY, his cousin
Enthusiastic

MR. PODGERS, the cheiromantist
Mysterious

HERR WINCKELKOPF, an anarchist
Artistic

The play should move briskly from scene to scene. Various possibilities exist for double-casting. *WEST MOON STREET* can be performed with or without an intermission.

ACT ONE

SCENE ONE

Lady Windermere's Drawing Room. A small table with chairs, and a few larger, more comfortable chairs. Off-stage, the sound of chatter from guests in other rooms. Entering the Drawing Room are **LADY WINDERMERE,** *a proud, extravagant woman of a certain age,* **LADY CLEM,** *an elderly dowager, and* **LORD ARTHUR** *and* **SYBIL MERTON,** *in their early twenties, dressed simply.*

LORD ARTHUR. This is one of your best nights, Lady Windermere

LADY WINDERMERE. All my lions are here!

LADY CLEM. Performing lions. Jumping through hoops at your request.

LORD ARTHUR. Must every gentleman kiss Sybil's hand?

LADY WINDERMERE. This is where they will begin, surely. (*to* **SYBIL**) Where they end depends on you, dear.

SYBIL smiles politely, **LORD ARTHUR** *is embarrassed.*

LORD ARTHUR. O, my.

LADY WINDERMERE. I am utterly devoted to Arthur, Sybil - even if he is a bit dull

SYBIL. I find Arthur quite diverting, actually.

LORD ARTHUR. Thank you, darling. I was, after all, at

Oxford.

LADY CLEM. Hush, boy! You must never mention that in polite society.

LADY WINDERMERE. (*to* **SYBIL**, *unconvincingly*) The peau de soie is enchanting on you, dear.

SYBIL. That's awfully kind, Lady Windermere.

LADY WINDERMERE. But I hoped you'd wear something – less conventional.

SYBIL. I must admit I feel out of place among such an exotic medley of people.

LORD ARTHUR. I've always seen a touch of Greek grace in Sybil's pose.

LADY CLEM. I abhor the Greeks. Change the topic at once.

> **SYBIL** *assists* **LADY CLEM** *into one of the comfortable chairs.*

LADY WINDERMERE. (*to* **SYBIL**)Enjoy this brief time, my dear. Soon you shall marry, and all pleasure will cease.

SYBIL. I trust that true pleasure shall <u>begin</u> on my wedding day.

LADY WINDERMERE. I speak from vast experience, Sybil.

SYBIL. Vast?

LORD ARTHUR. (*to* **SYBIL**) Despite various matrimonial defeats, Lady Windermere's search for gratification continues to thrive.

LADY WINDERMERE. It is the secret to remaining young.

LADY CLEM. Indeed it is. I attribute my remarkable fitness to unstinting personal indulgence. Sybil, have you ordered the cake? (*she emits odd guttural sounds*) I'm erupting. Arthur, fetch my fan.

> **LORD ARTHUR** *retrieves* **LADY CLEM'S** *fan.*

LORD ARTHUR. Here it is, Lady Clem. Shall I cool you awhile?

LADY CLEM. Be gone.

> **LADY CLEM** *grabs the fan and cools herself haughtily.*

LADY WINDERMERE. Before your wedding, you must lunch with me, Sybil. We shall talk of frocks and husbands.

SYBIL. My frocks and your husbands, presumably.

LADY CLEM. I doubt you will be of any assistance regarding the latter, Gladys. I remained devoted to Paisley my entire life, while you supplanted three spouses –

LORD ARTHUR. – and countless lovers –

LADY WINDERMERE. – which qualifies me to speak on the matter.

LORD ARTHUR. That is why London society has never ceased to talk scandal about you.

SYBIL. I am averse to scandal.

LADY WINDERMERE. While I feel it is my Duty to create an atmosphere in which scandal can thrive.

LORD ARTHUR. I so admire a person with a Duty.

> **JANE PERCY**, *a gauche, overdressed young woman barges into the room.*

JANE. Lady Windermere, your reception is ever so stimulating – particularly compared with the dreary affairs in Chichester!

SYBIL. You should visit London more often, Jane. Society delights you so. (*to* **LORD ARTHUR**) I, on the other hand, harbor pastoral longings.

LADY WINDERMERE. I'm sure there's a medicine for that.

JANE. Princess Sophia is bedecked with the most enormous emeralds I've ever seen –

LADY CLEM. To disguise her increasingly <u>enormous</u> physique.

JANE. – and a bevy of bishops is chasing a prima donna from room to room!

LADY CLEM. However do they manage to give chase in those flamboyant ecclesiastic vestments?

LADY WINDERMERE. They are irrepressible. Which is why I invite them.

JANE. (*apprehensively*) What if Papa were to see this?

LADY WINDERMERE. Apparently the Archdeacon prefers to admonish sin in Chichester than to commit it in London.

LADY CLEM. Are they such wicked heathens out there that God's work occupies him so exhaustively?

JANE. Papa finds displeasure with society. He prefers to spend evenings alone in his study, writing sermons. From nine in the post meridian until every clock strikes eleven, he must not be disturbed.

LORD ARTHUR. Every clock, cousin?

JANE. Really, Arthur. You should visit us more often. Papa has an immense collection of timepieces.

LADY WINDERMERE. Whatever for? He has no social engagements.

JANE. Indeed, he shuns society, which he believes has become quite irreligious.

LADY WINDERMERE. It has, mercifully.

LADY CLEM. Particularly the clergy.

JANE. While I, despite Papa's protestations, struggle desperately to keep up with the fashions.

LADY WINDERMERE. Your desperate effort does not go unnoticed, dear.

JANE. Papa feels that lower class women should not try to dress like the upper class.

LORD ARTHUR. How was that?

SYBIL. The Archdeacon holds this opinion regarding the dressing habits of ladies?

JANE. I've extrapolated it from his sermons.

SYBIL. (*amused*) I see.

JANE. Lady Clem, do you agree that it is nonsense for destitute women to wear pretty things?

LADY CLEM. Absolutely. Their wardrobe should be repellent. It is only proper.

SYBIL. I must say I find it silly, this anxiety about dress.

LADY WINDERMERE. Ornamentation is the only issue in modern society worth being anxious about.

SYBIL. Surely there are more important matters in this world.

JANE. And the next, according to Papa.

LADY WINDERMERE. Ah yes, the next. I am insufficiently reflective of the next world, being preoccupied as I am with this one.

JANE. Papa believes that we live in an age of unbelief. He is persuaded that his solemn Duty is to bring God to the godless.

LORD ARTHUR. I've searched eagerly for a Duty, but to no avail.

LADY CLEM. A gentleman must have a Duty, Arthur. It is essential to his moral character. Makes no difference what it is. Smoking, for example, is quite good.

LORD ARTHUR. Has your heartburn improved, Lady Clem?

LADY CLEM. If you persist in prying into my personal affairs, I shall remove you from my will.

SYBIL. (*to* **LADY CLEM**) My dear, Arthur was only interested in whether –

LADY CLEM. Cease!

JANE. Sybil, would you say it is true that the ladies in London wear bows now, and frilled underskirts?

SYBIL. I am uncertain, dear. Perhaps you should look to your father's sermons.

LADY WINDERMERE. The reception beckons, Jane Percy. Seek your answers there.

JANE hurries off.

LORD ARTHUR. She is a high-spirited girl.

SYBIL. It must be the Chichester air.

LADY CLEM. Fresh air is bad for the constitution.

LADY WINDERMERE. And the complexion.

LADY CLEM. I attribute my remarkable fitness to a complete isolation from nature. (*she emits guttural sounds*) I'm erupting again. Fetch my medicines!

*SYBIL retrieves **LADY CLEM**'s medicines, and pours a glass of water.*

SYBIL. Here you are, dear.

LADY CLEM. Sybil, your interest in my well-being has conspicuously flagged. You have not been at my home in weeks. I suppose my nephew is to blame – he hasn't visited in years.

LADY CLEM swallows a handful of medicines.

SYBIL. I apologize, Lady Clem. We are overrun with preparations for our wedding.

LADY CLEM. Your wedding? Rubbish!

LADY WINDERMERE. Rubbish precisely. And now, the time has come for my cheiromantist.

SYBIL. A cheiromantist. How daring.

LORD ARTHUR. What exactly is a (*struggling with the pronunciation*) cheir-o-man –

LADY CLEM. (*authoritatively*) The same thing as a chiropodist.

LADY WINDERMERE. In fact, Podgers is a palmist. He's my new little pet.

LADY CLEM. (*suspiciously*) He tells fortunes, I suppose?

LADY WINDERMERE. And misfortunes. Any amount of them. Recently, he suggested that if my thumb had been the least bit longer, I should have gone into a convent.

LADY CLEM. Must be a foreigner.

LADY WINDERMERE. Next year it seems, I am in great danger, both by land and sea. So I plan to live in a balloon and every evening, have my dinner drawn up in a basket.

SYBIL. This was inscribed on the palm your hand?

LADY WINDERMERE. Or my little finger, I forget which.

LADY CLEM. You are tempting Providence, Gladys.

LORD ARTHUR. (*to* **LADY CLEM**, *lightly*) My dear aunt, surely by this time, Providence can resist temptation.

LADY CLEM. (*enraged*) Oxonian!

SYBIL. Arthur meant no disrespect. He was –

LORD ARTHUR. – I was often distracted during my years there.

LADY CLEM. (*interrupting, to* **LORD ARTHUR**) Distracted from learning? What should have distracted you from your learning?

LORD ARTHUR. Nicknames.

LADY CLEM. Nicknames?

LORD ARTHUR. I spent a good deal of time at Oxford coining nicknames for my classmates.

LADY CLEM. (*a beat, then turns to* **SYBIL**) I beg you, my dear – reconsider this union.

LADY WINDERMERE. Which is precisely why I invited Mr. Podgers. He shall tell us if Arthur will make a good husband, or if, before the year is out, we should expect to find Sybil floating in the Thames.

SYBIL. O, my.

LORD ARTHUR. Bring the man forth that he may put the matter to rest.

SYBIL. Must we, dear?

LADY WINDERMERE. Everyone should have their hands told, Sybil – so as to know what not to do.

SYBIL. And you mind this man's advice?

LADY WINDERMERE. (*a beat, then*) Indubitably. Arthur, fetch Podgers at once.

SYBIL. Please, Arthur – I beg you.

> **LORD ARTHUR,** *standing between* **SYBIL** *and* **LADY WINDERMERE,** *considers a moment, then speaks.*

LORD ARTHUR. (*to* **LADY WINDERMERE**) How shall I recognize him?

> **LADY WINDERMERE** *beams.* **SYBIL** *turns away dismayed.*

LADY WINDERMERE. Well, he is not a bit like a cheiromantist.

Not at all esoteric or romantic-looking.

LORD ARTHUR. What is he like, Lady Windermere?

LADY WINDERMERE. Something between a gnome and a country attorney.

LORD ARTHUR. The particulars of his physical aspect would expedite the search.

LADY WINDERMERE. He is round as an acorn –

LORD ARTHUR. Aha!

LADY WINDERMERE. – and does not come up very far from the ground.

SYBIL. (*to* **LORD ARTHUR,** *sardonically*) That should narrow the field for you, dear.

> **LORD ARTHUR** *hurries from the room.*

LADY CLEM. Gladys, you invite far too many people to your receptions who never look like what they are. It is most aggravating.

LADY WINDERMERE. Am I to blame if my pianists look like anarchists, and my anarchists look exactly like pianists?

SYBIL. What, pray, does an anarchist look like?

LADY WINDERMERE. Invariably, they have long, slender fingers. Do you remember Herr Winckelkopf, to whom I introduced you earlier?

SYBIL. That rumpled fellow? I assumed he was a solicitor.

LADY WINDERMERE. Anarchist. He's blown up ever so many people.

SYBIL. O! no. Why ever did you invite him?

LADY WINDERMERE. To fill out my reception's criminal quota.

LADY CLEM. What is one to do in an age when solicitors are indistinguishable from anarchists?

SYBIL. Open one's correspondence very carefully.

> **MR. PODGERS** *and* **LORD ARTHUR** *enter the room.* **MR. PODGERS** *is short, and exudes charm. He speaks with a "foreign" accent.*

LADY WINDERMERE. Ah, here's Podgers, my pet cheiromantist!

MR. PODGERS. (*bows formally and kisses her hand*) Good evening, my dear Lady Windermere.

> **JANE** *barges in.*

JANE. What's going on in here!? (*whispering loudly to* **SYBIL**) Who's that teeny creature?

SYBIL. Mr. Podgers is a cheiromantist, Jane.

JANE. What in the wide world is that?

SYBIL. He will be examining palms and telling futures, apparently.

LADY WINDERMERE. Now Podgers, I want you to read Sybil's hand.

MR. PODGERS. I would be delighted. Miss Merton? (*indicating the small table and chairs*)

SYBIL. Thank you. I couldn't.

LADY WINDERMERE. Sybil, remove your gloves and sit down.

SYBIL. Thank you, no.

MR. PODGERS. Are you so certain of your future?

SYBIL. I am, yes.

LORD ARTHUR. It's for amusement, darling.

SYBIL. I don't think it's quite right.

LADY WINDERMERE. Nothing amusing ever is.

JANE. Go on, Sybil! Give it a whirl!

SYBIL. (*entreatingly*) Arthur –

LORD ARTHUR. Sybil and I shall be spectators, Lady Windermere.

JANE. Let the Lilliputian tell <u>my</u> hand!

LADY WINDERMERE. Whatever for? Do you have a secret past, Jane Percy?

JANE. No, but I hope to have a wicked future!

> **MR. PODGERS** *sits at a small table.*

LADY WINDERMERE. I suppose this will have to do.

> **JANE** *plops down in the chair opposite* **MR. PODGERS**.

MR. PODGERS. Not a reserved nature –

SYBIL. (*mock sincerity*) The man is gifted, Lady Windermere! Wherever did you find him?

> **JANE** *thrusts her hand in* **MR. PODGERS***' face. He sniffs it.*

MR. PODGERS. Great love of animals?

JANE. Quite true! We keep two dozen collie dogs in Chichester. I'd turn our house into a menagerie if Papa would let me. I love a good romp with a collie dog!

LADY WINDERMERE. That sounds unhygienic, Jane.

JANE. Go on, Mr. Podgers. Am I destined for marriage?

MR. PODGERS. It is not entirely out of the question that a slight chance of such an unlikely arrangement might be considered a remote possibility, yes.

JANE. Will my husband be lean or spherical?

LADY WINDERMERE. (*impatiently*) Read some other hands

for us, Podgers.

JANE. (*to* **MR. PODGERS,** *sweetly*) Tell me, little runt – what is most in vogue nowadays in ladies' undergarments?

LADY WINDERMERE. Consult the bishops, dear. It's their area of expertise.

JANE *flees the room.*

LADY CLEM. (*craving attention*) We British revere our ancestors, sir.

LADY WINDERMERE. Once they're in the grave.

LADY CLEM. (*to* **MR. PODGERS,** *removing a glove*) Perhaps in the country of your origin –

SYBIL. – wherever that may be –

LADY CLEM. – dowagers are tossed out like torn lace.

LORD ARTHUR. Come, Lady Clem, I see how eager you are to have Mr. Podgers read your hand.

LADY CLEM. (*coyly*) I mustn't!

MR. PODGERS. We shall see if her mountain of the moon is larger than yours, Lady Windermere.

LADY CLEM. (*doesn't like the sound of it*) Mountain of the moon? I'm sure there is nothing of the kind in <u>my</u> hand. (**LADY CLEM** *sits in the chair opposite* **MR. PODGERS,** *offering her hand.*) Mr. Podgers, do you see any – lunar elevations?

MR. PODGERS. The mountain of the moon is not developed.

LADY CLEM. (*pleased*) As I suspected.

MR. PODGERS. The line of life, however, is excellent. Three distinct lines on the rascette. You will live to a great age, Lady Clem.

SYBIL. What a remarkable prediction!

LORD ARTHUR. (*innocently*) Live to what age, exactly?

LADY CLEM. Are you depraved, man? Sybil, I implore you – cancel the nuptials at once.

SYBIL. (*lightly*) I am resolute, Lady Clem.

MR. PODGERS. Line of ambition – very modest. Line of intellect – not exaggerated –

LADY CLEM. (*proudly*) Indeed. Women should avoid intellect entirely.

MR. PODGERS. Line of heart –

LADY CLEM. (*coyly*) You mustn't be indiscreet, young man.

LADY WINDERMERE. Nothing would please me more.

MR. PODGERS. I am sorry to disappoint you, Lady Windermere, but I see great permanence of affection here.

LADY CLEM. (*to the heavens*) Paisley. Paisley! Are you listening to this adorable alien?

MR. PODGERS. Even following her husband's untimely death.

LORD ARTHUR. What do you know of Uncle's death?

MR. PODGERS. (*without looking at* **LADY CLEM'S** *palm*) Died in a shipwreck. He was a Conservative, very punctual. Had a severe illness at the age of eighteen. Was left a fortune when he was thirty. Great aversion to radicals and felines.

LORD ARTHUR. Uncle Paisley detested cats. This is extraordinary!

SYBIL. Cheiromancy is a dubious science, Arthur. One ought not to be so susceptible.

LORD ARTHUR. Even the Greeks placed their trust in prophecies, Sybil.

LADY CLEM. Enough of the Greeks! Pray go on, Mr.

Podgers. You're doing brilliantly! What does my pinkie portend?

LADY CLEM *wags her little finger at* **MR. PODGERS**.

MR. PODGERS. Financial prudence is not foremost among your attributes, Lady Clem.

LADY CLEM. (*proudly*) Indulgence is the one thing this dreadful civilization allows us, and I feel it my Duty to exploit it to the maximum.

LADY WINDERMERE. Indeed, one's life must be strewn with amenities.

MR. PODGERS. (*examining her thumb*) What have we here?

LADY WINDERMERE. Something shocking, I beg you.

MR. PODGERS. I see that your husband's finances were entirely depleted. Many held that you, Lady Clem, were responsible.

LADY CLEM. What's this?

MR. PODGERS. Some have gone so far as to suggest that you secreted away your husband's fortune during his lifetime –

LADY CLEM. Paisley, ignore this homunculus!

MR. PODGERS. – only to dissipate it after his death.

LADY CLEM. (*pulling her hand away*) You are quite wrong, Mr. Podgers.

SYBIL. Indeed you are, sir.

LADY CLEM. Sybil, my glove.

> **SYBIL** *hands* **LADY CLEM** *her glove. She puts it on, then slides her hands under her thighs.*

LORD ARTHUR. Mr. Podgers, would you be so kind as to tell my palm?

WEST MOON STREET 21

SYBIL. Arthur!

LADY WINDERMERE. (*to* **LORD ARTHUR**, *dismissively*) My wish is that Podgers unearth scandal, dear. That is not feasible in your case. Sybil, are <u>you</u> persuaded?

SYBIL. I am without scandal, Lady Windermere.

LADY WINDERMERE. You mustn't be so certain, dear.

SYBIL. I am, nonetheless.

MR. PODGERS. I warn you beforehand, sir – I will hold nothing back.

LADY WINDERMERE *looks* **MR. PODGERS** *in the eye.*

LORD ARTHUR. Nor do I expect you to.

LADY WINDERMERE. If he discovers that you are prone to gluttony, or have a wife living in Bayswater, Sybil shall certainly hear all about it.

SYBIL. (*to* **LORD ARTHUR**, *amused*) Anywhere but Bayswater, dear.

LORD ARTHUR. I am not afraid. Sybil knows me as well as I know myself.

LADY WINDERMERE. Pity. The proper basis for marriage is mutual misunderstanding.

SYBIL. I must say, I was unaware you were so cynical, Lady Windermere.

LADY WINDERMERE. I am not cynical. I merely have experience – which is the same thing.

    LORD ARTHUR *sits opposite* **MR. PODGERS**.

LORD ARTHUR. I am ready, sir.

    MR. PODGERS *takes* **LORD ARTHUR'S** *hand.* **MR. PODGERS**' *expression turns suddenly serious. He takes out a handkerchief and wipes his brow.* **LORD ARTHUR**

stares at him. Tense silence.

LORD ARTHUR. I am waiting, Mr. Podgers.

LADY CLEM. Lord Arthur will suffer severely for his persecution of the elderly. Am I correct?

> **LORD ARTHUR** *doesn't answer. After a few moments,*
> **MR. PODGERS** *releases* **LORD ARTHUR'S** *hand, takes his other hand and stares at it closely. Appearing frightened by what he sees, he releases the hand quickly.*

LADY WINDERMERE. We are waiting, Podgers.

MR. PODGERS. (*to* **LORD ARTHUR**) Within the month, you will lose a relative.

LADY WINDERMERE. Congratulations, Arthur.

LADY CLEM. Sybil, you should have a black silk on hand just in case – it does nicely for the church – (*suddenly apprehensive*) Hallo – which relative?

LADY WINDERMERE. (*to* **MR. PODGERS**) Is that all you can tell us?

MR. PODGERS. (*forcing a smile*) It is the hand of a charming young man.

LADY CLEM. I don't think a husband should be too charming. (*fondly*) My dear Paisley was utterly bereft of charm!

LORD ARTHUR. Is this the entire forecast, sir?

> **MR. PODGERS** *doesn't answer.* **LORD ARTHUR** *stares at him.*

LADY WINDERMERE. We have learned nothing at all disgraceful. I am displeased. Let's go to supper.

SYBIL. Lady Clem, I'm sure your ancient bones are weary and you must hurry home.

LADY CLEM. Not a chance. What's being served, Gladys? I'm ravished.

SYBIL. Perhaps you mean ravenous, dear?

LADY CLEM. I must eat. Am I understood?

LADY WINDERMERE. My lions are sure to have eaten everything up by now – but there may still be soup.

LADY CLEM. (*with disgust*) Soup?

LADY WINDERMERE. Francois makes an excellent vegetable broth.

LADY CLEM. His last soup was disgusting.

LADY WINDERMERE. He's been experimenting with spices from the contagious continents.

LADY CLEM. I must have cake!

> **SYBIL** *helps* **LADY CLEM** *toward the door.*

SYBIL. (*to* **LORD ARTHUR**) Won't you join us, darling?

LORD ARTHUR. In a moment.

LADY WINDERMERE. Come along, Podgers. You've had your chance. I shall have to invite a telepathist to my next reception.

> **LADY WINDERMERE, LADY CLEM** *and* **SYBIL** *exit.* **MR. PODGERS** *follows.*

MR. PODGERS. Good evening, sir.

LORD ARTHUR. Mr. Podgers, I insist that you give me a straightforward answer to the question I am to put to you.

MR. PODGERS. We mustn't keep the ladies waiting.

LORD ARTHUR. (*extending his arm to stop* **PODGERS**) Tell me what you saw in my palm.

MR. PODGERS. You believe I saw something more than I

told you?

LORD ARTHUR. I'm certain you did, and I insist that you tell me what it was.

MR. PODGERS. Sir, I cannot.

LORD ARTHUR. I will send a cheque for one hundred pounds tomorrow.

MR. PODGERS *stops, then turns toward* **LORD ARTHUR.**

LORD ARTHUR. What is your club?

MR. PODGERS. I have no club – that is to say, not at present. Allow me to give you my card.

He takes a card from his pocket and hands it to **LORD ARTHUR.**

LORD ARTHUR. (*reading*) Mr. Septimus R. Podgers. Professional Cheiromantist. 103a West Moon Street.

MR. PODGERS. Are you absolutely certain you want to know?

LORD ARTHUR. Absolutely. But you mustn't tell another soul.

MR. PODGERS. Of course not. Our discussion is privileged.

LORD ARTHUR. Then be quick, sir. Speak!

SCENE TWO

Lord Arthur's Rooms. A writing table and a chair. On the table is a framed photograph of **SYBIL**. **CHARLES,** **LORD ARTHUR'S** *valet, stands behind* **LORD ARTHUR,** *who paces.*

LORD ARTHUR. Murder!

CHARLES. I beg your pardon, my lord?

LORD ARTHUR. Murder, Charles! He saw it in my hand. The palmist predicts that I will commit a murder.

CHARLES. (*lightly*) He is an imposter, sir.

LORD ARTHUR. He knew all about Uncle Paisley. I was skeptical till then. But the man was aware of every detail, Charles, right down to the cats!

CHARLES. Surely he secured this information in advance.

LORD ARTHUR. Lady Windermere puts her absolute trust in his predictions.

CHARLES. Women like that have one desire, my lord.

LORD ARTHUR. What is that, Charles?

CHARLES. (*with disdain*) Amusement.

> **LORD ARTHUR** *removes* **MR. PODGERS**' *card from his pocket and hands it to* **CHARLES**.

LORD ARTHUR. Doesn't belong to a club. What do you make of that?

CHARLES. He is no gentleman, sir. And it would be wise to ignore his prognostication.

> **CHARLES** *studies the card before putting it in his pocket.*

LORD ARTHUR. You don't understand, Charles. I am a man of birth and fortune. I have lived a life free from sordid care. Suddenly, for the first time in my life, Destiny has been thrust upon me.

CHARLES. You have been wandering the streets all night, sir. It would be wise to take toddy and have a good lie-down.

LORD ARTHUR. Could some sin be written on my hand? (*staring at his hand*) Some blood-red sign of crime?

> **LORD ARTHUR** *thrusts his hand in front of* **CHARLES**, *who glances at it casually.*

CHARLES. Your hand is a tabula rasa, my lord.

LORD ARTHUR. I feel no better than a chessman being moved about by an unseen power.

CHARLES. You have a finely wrought nature, sir.

LORD ARTHUR. Actors are so fortunate. They can choose whether they will make merry or shed tears. But real people are different.

CHARLES. We apply less rouge?

LORD ARTHUR. We are forced to perform parts for which we have no qualifications.

CHARLES. The world is a stage, and the play is badly cast.

LORD ARTHUR. Perhaps, Charles, we are merely puppets in an endless pantomime.

CHARLES. I would find that fatiguing, sir.

LORD ARTHUR. Whatever am I to do?

CHARLES. You should bathe.

LORD ARTHUR. How monstrous this all seems!

CHARLES. Permit me to bring you a cup of chocolate.

> **CHARLES** *moves to exit as an anguished* **LORD ARTHUR** *crosses to the window.* **CHARLES** *stops to watch him.*

LORD ARTHUR. It is almost dawn, Charles. The wagons are on their way to Covent Garden. What a strange London they see, these rustics. Free from care and responsibility. I envy them their ignorance.

CHARLES. You are very young, sir.

> **LORD ARTHUR** *picks up the picture of Sybil.*

LORD ARTHUR. Is Sybil Merton not perfectly proportioned, Charles?

CHARLES. She is, indeed. A rare thing in an age when most women are oversized or insignificant.

LORD ARTHUR. What happiness could there be for us when at any moment, I may be called upon to carry out the prophecy Fate has written in my hand? (*puts the picture down*) The marriage must be postponed at once.

CHARLES. Patience, my lord.

LORD ARTHUR. I have no right to marry Sybil until I have committed the murder.

CHARLES. (*concealing his alarm*) Sir?

LORD ARTHUR. (*eagerly*) It is my Duty, Charles. The opportunity I craved. I recognize it now!

CHARLES. Your reasoning has obviously been impared by the soup at Lady Windermere's reception.

LORD ARTHUR. It's not the soup, Charles. Once my Task is accomplished, I shall be able to look Sybil in the eye.

CHARLES. Task, sir?

LORD ARTHUR. Only then will I stand with her before the altar. But I must complete my Mission first.

CHARLES. A Mission provoked by the augury of a scoundrel.

LORD ARTHUR. There is no other course. It is a sacrifice I must make for Sybil.

CHARLES. You have convinced yourself.

LORD ARTHUR. I have merely chosen between living for myself, and living for another.

CHARLES. I have also made that choice.

> **LORD ARTHUR** *looks* **CHARLES** *in the eye.*

CHARLES. Whom then, my lord?

LORD ARTHUR. What do you mean, Charles?

CHARLES. Whom do you intend to murder?

LORD ARTHUR. I hadn't thought of that. But I'm sure it's quite necessary.

CHARLES. I'm afraid so, sir. Like the religions of the Pagan world, murder requires a victim as well as a priest.

LORD ARTHUR. Yes, I see. A victim. And I was considering only my own sacrifice.

CHARLES. Do you have enemies, Lord Arthur?

LORD ARTHUR. Surely this is an inappropriate time for the gratification of any personal pique.

CHARLES. Indeed, it is a grave matter.

LORD ARTHUR. Poor choice of words, Charles.

CHARLES. My apologies, sir.

LORD ARTHUR. Why don't we make out a list of acquaintances on a sheet of notepaper?

CHARLES. May I offer a suggestion as to "victim," my lord?

LORD ARTHUR. That was brisk. Whom, Charles?

CHARLES. Lady Clementina Beauchamp.

LORD ARTHUR. Lady Clem!? But she's my Aunt. I've always been fond of the old dear, even if she misreads, and consequently disapproves of my conduct.

CHARLES. She is quite advanced in years, sir.

LORD ARTHUR. To be sure. One foot astride the grave. Nonetheless, I admit to a certain hesitancy regarding the disposal of a relation.

CHARLES. Being her nephew, you may visit Lady Clem when you will without arousing suspicion.

LORD ARTHUR. As an infrequent guest, I dare say a visit from me would, in fact, arouse Lady Clem's suspicion. But I'm certain I could persuade her of my sincerity.

CHARLES. Of that there is no doubt.

LORD ARTHUR. (*a beat, then*) You are correct, Charles. Lady Clem is just the right person to do away with. That's settled, then.

CHARLES. How, sir?

LORD ARTHUR. What do you mean, "how," Charles?

CHARLES. How shall you do away with her?

LORD ARTHUR. Oh, I see, yes. Well, first off, any course that involves personal violence is extremely distasteful to me.

CHARLES. And to all Englishmen.

LORD ARTHUR. I will not allow of a method to murder that might cause scandal.

CHARLES. Admirable.

LORD ARTHUR. And of course I must consider Sybil's parents. They are old-fashioned people, and would object to anything that might attract public atten –

CHARLES. (*interrupting*) I have a suggestion as to "how," my Lord.

LORD ARTHUR. As to "how," Charles?

CHARLES. Yes, sir.

LORD ARTHUR. How, Charles?

CHARLES. Poison.

LORD ARTHUR. That is very good, Charles. Poison is safe and sure. It is also quiet. And poison would eliminate the necessity for painful scenes, to which I have a rooted objection.

CHARLES. As do all Englishmen.

LORD ARTHUR. But I know nothing of chemistry. I wish I had been more attentive to those lectures at Oxford.

CHARLES. A suggestion, sir.

LORD ARTHUR. A suggestion as to "which poison," Charles?

CHARLES. Yes, sir.

LORD ARTHUR. Which, Charles?

CHARLES. Aconitine. It is swift – indeed, almost immediate in its effect. It is perfectly painless, and when taken in the form of a gelatin capsule, not unpalatable.

LORD ARTHUR. All that, you say. And where will you get such a poison?

CHARLES. Pestle and Humby's, the chemists on St. James Street.

LORD ARTHUR. Won't Mr. Pestle and Mr. Humby be surprised at the order?

CHARLES. I will explain that I am obliged by my master to put down a large Norwegian Mastiff, as it has already bitten the coachman twice and exhibits signs of incipient rabies.

LORD ARTHUR. Charles, it is impossible for me to express my gratitude toward you at this moment.

CHARLES. It is my Duty, sir.

LORD ARTHUR *sits at his table and writes a cheque.*

LORD ARTHUR. I must settle with the cheiromantist. Here is a cheque for one hundred pounds, payable to the order of Mr. Septimus R. Podgers. Before visiting the chemists, take this to West Moon Street.

CHARLES. 103a.

LORD ARTHUR. I shall go to my club for a lemon and soda, then to the Bonbon Shoppe on Bond Street to purchase a bonbonniere for the poison capsule.

CHARLES. Very thoughtful.

LORD ARTHUR. But first – to Sybil. Whatever shall I tell her!?

SCENE THREE

St. James Park. **LORD ARTHUR** *paces anxiously near a bench. He is carrying a bouquet. After a few moments,* **SYBIL** *arrives. He runs into her arms.*

LORD ARTHUR. My darling! A single night without you is too much to bear.

SYBIL. Those nights grow fewer in number.

LORD ARTHUR. Soon I shall never again wait to hold you.

SYBIL. Unless of course there are bishops afoot. Then you must queue up.

LORD ARTHUR. (*clutching her tighter*) Sybil! My own one!

SYBIL. Arthur, you must release me, or we shall expose ourselves to censure from the nursemaids.

> **LORD ARTHUR** *releases* **SYBIL** *and hands her the bouquet.*

LORD ARTHUR. For you, my love.

SYBIL. Narcissi! Such lovely petals. (*she kisses his cheek*) How divine of you to suggest that we meet here. St. James is enchanting in the spring. And considerably less tumultuous than my residence at the moment.

LORD ARTHUR. I thought it best to avoid your parents.

SYBIL. Indeed. The preparations have hurled them into frenzy.

LORD ARTHUR. (*sullenly*) Our wedding. Yes.

> **LORD ARTHUR** *sits on the bench, and* **SYBIL** *sits close to him.*

SYBIL. You look awfully tired. Is that hideous soup having an after-effect?

LORD ARTHUR. It's not the soup, Sybil.

SYBIL. What's troubling you?

LORD ARTHUR. (*a beat, then*) Sybil, I adore you. You are more to me than all the world.

SYBIL. You sound as if you were about to propose. I am yours, darling. You may abandon this idle line of chatter.

LORD ARTHUR. I am filled with a terrible pity.

SYBIL. Whatever for?

LORD ARTHUR. I cannot bear what I must say.

SYBIL. Arthur, what is wrong?

LORD ARTHUR. Sybil, my love. I have been put into a position of terrible difficulty, from which Duty will not allow me to recede.

SYBIL. What has happened?

LORD ARTHUR. Our marriage must be put off for the present.

SYBIL. (*a beat, then sweetly*) And I am Queen Victoria.

LORD ARTHUR. Until I get rid of – that is – until I can eliminate – that is, until I can – undo a severe entanglement, I am not a free man.

SYBIL. Are you in earnest? Arthur, I don't understand.

LORD ARTHUR. How could you?

SYBIL. If you were to explain the particulars to me –

LORD ARTHUR. I cannot.

SYBIL. Then you must undo this entanglement before our wedding date.

LORD ARTHUR. Trust me, Sybil. Our future is secure. Everything will come right in the end.

SYBIL. That is unlikely. Father is sure to call off the marriage.

LORD ARTHUR. I will write him a letter – a firm, manly letter. I shall explain the absolute necessity to postpone the wedding, and my unswerving commitment to marriage a later date.

SYBIL. Is Lady Windermere's suspicion correct – do you have a wife in Bayswater?

LORD ARTHUR. There has never been, and there will never be another woman in my life – in Bayswater or anywhere else.

SYBIL. (*a beat, then*) Only last night, you said, "Sybil knows me as well as I know myself." This afternoon, Arthur, it is quite clear that I do not know you at all.

> **SYBIL** *hands the bouquet back to* **LORD ARTHUR**.

LORD ARTHUR. What am I to do!?

SYBIL. What you promised. Marry me.

LORD ARTHUR. I shall.

SYBIL. On schedule!

LORD ARTHUR. That I cannot. But very soon, we will – reschedule.

SYBIL. There is no such word.

LORD ARTHUR. (*sincerely*) There is now.

SYBIL. O, Arthur. You no longer love me, is that it?

LORD ARTHUR. Look at you – with your delicate head drooped to one side, as if your reed-like neck couldn't bear the burden of so much beauty. (*he embraces her, and weakens*) O, Sybil.

SYBIL. (*hopefully*) Yes, Arthur?

> **LORD ARTHUR** *jumps up suddenly and moves a distance away.*

LORD ARTHUR. I mustn't! I have a Duty!

SYBIL. Indeed you have – to me!

LORD ARTHUR. But it would be wrong to allow my tender feelings for you to dissuade me from my Mission.

SYBIL. How could it be wrong?

LORD ARTHUR. When my Task is complete, I am yours forever. But to marry before then, my love, would be unfair to you.

> **SYBIL** *looks up, yielding.* **LORD ARTHUR** *hands her the bouquet.*

SYBIL. (*a beat, then*) Your Duty must be formidable indeed. Now you have my pity, Arthur.

LORD ARTHUR. The Mission I undertake is for the better good.

SYBIL. May I know the nature of your Mission?

LORD ARTHUR. Sybil, you may not.

SYBIL. May I one day?

LORD ARTHUR. Late one summer night perhaps, when our children are nestled in their beds.

SYBIL. (*passionately*) O, Arthur.

LORD ARTHUR. I must leave you now. Will you wait, Sybil?

SYBIL. What shall I say to the milliners?

LORD ARTHUR. Promise me you will wait.

SYBIL. It is my Duty, sir.

LORD ARTHUR. Then tell the milliners we shall yet require their services!

> **LORD ARTHUR** *kisses her on the cheek and runs off.* **SYBIL** *sits alone, confused.*

SCENE FOUR

Lady Clem's Parlor. She lies on a divan, covered in flannels. Books, medicines and other items clutter every exposed surface. **LORD ARTHUR** *enters.*

LADY CLEM. Well, young man, have you come to apologize for your brutal mistreatment of me?

LORD ARTHUR. That is among my objectives, yes.

LADY CLEM. What has taken you so long?

LORD ARTHUR. The reception was only last night, Lady Clem. But so much is astir.

LADY CLEM. I haven't the faintest idea why young people make such a fuss about marriage. What's a wedding but dresses and vows and the rest of it?

LORD ARTHUR. And of course, the cake.

LADY CLEM. Ah, yes. The cake!

LORD ARTHUR. Despite a bustling schedule, I did not neglect my dear aunt.

LADY CLEM. I suppose that you were about all day long with Miss Sybil Merton, buying chiffons and talking nonsense?

LORD ARTHUR. I visited with Sybil for a brief moment only, this noon in St. James Park.

LADY CLEM. In my day, we never dreamed of billing and cooing in public – or in private, for that matter. (*a beat, then*) We were circumcised.

LORD ARTHUR. Surely you mean circum<u>spect</u>, my dear Aunt.

LADY CLEM. Have you come here to correct my phraseology?

LORD ARTHUR. You may trust that my behavior with Sybil was most proper. And now she belongs entirely to her milliners.

LADY CLEM. Is that the reason you chose to visit an ugly old woman like myself?

LORD ARTHUR. You look splendid, my dear. Like a Titian.

LADY CLEM. (*flattery moves her to self-pity*) I am alone, Arthur. A poor, rheumatic creature, with a false front and a bad temper. Were it not for Jane Percy, who sends me all the worst French novels she can find, I don't think I could get through the day.

LORD ARTHUR. Has your doctor paid a visit of late?

LADY CLEM. Doctors are of no use at all, nephew. Not even the most obsequious has cured my heartburn.

LORD ARTHUR. I've brought you something for that, Lady Clem.

LADY CLEM. (*eagerly*) You've become a chemist?

LORD ARTHUR. Heavens, no. I did glance through "Pharmacopoeia" at my club, but I found all the symbols disorienting.

LADY CLEM. The truth is, although I hate doctors, I adore medicines!

LORD ARTHUR. This is a wonderful gelatin capsule, invented by an American.

LADY CLEM. The Americans invented the steam engine, did they not? I abhor the steam engine.

LORD ARTHUR. I believe they modified the British design.

LADY CLEM. To make it faster and cheaper, no doubt.

LORD ARTHUR. They do have a few awfully good things in America, Auntie.

LADY CLEM. That is unlikely. After all, they are the people responsible for the artificial leg.

LORD ARTHUR. Is that so?

LADY CLEM. The artificial leg is absurd, Arthur. Anyone who loses a leg should be isolated from society – and not rewarded with a wooden substitute.

LORD ARTHUR. There is nothing at all absurd about this medicine, Lady Clem. I assure you it is a perfect cure. You must promise to try it.

> **LORD ARTHUR** *takes a small silver box out of his pocket and hands it to* **LADY CLEM**.

LADY CLEM. What a charming bonbonnierre, Arthur.

LORD ARTHUR. A token of my regard.

LADY CLEM. Very appropriate. And inside is the capsule? (*eagerly opening the box*) Hallo – a bonbon!

LORD ARTHUR. That is most definitely not a bonbon, Lady Clem.

> **LADY CLEM** *removes the capsule.*

LADY CLEM. It looks scrumptious. I shall have it at once!

> **LORD ARTHUR** *grabs her by the hand.*

LORD ARTHUR. You mustn't do anything of the kind!

LADY CLEM. Calm yourself, boy. The variety of medicines I have consumed are too numerous to be catalogued, even in your "Pharmacopoeia."

LORD ARTHUR. But this is – this is a homeopathic medicine, Lady Clem. If you take it without having heartburn, it will do you no end of harm.

LADY CLEM. What manner of harm?

LORD ARTHUR. I'm not certain.

LADY CLEM. I suppose this is an American theory.

LORD ARTHUR. Wait until you have an attack and then take it. You will be astonished at the result.

LADY CLEM. It looks lovely!

She moves the capsule toward her mouth, but notices **LORD ARTHUR** *ready to pounce.*

LADY CLEM. (*disappointed*) However, if you insist, I shall save it until my next episode.

She returns the capsule to the bonbonniere.

LORD ARTHUR. And when will that be?

LADY CLEM. One never knows.

LORD ARTHUR. Will it be soon?

LADY CLEM. What is your inference, sir?

LORD ARTHUR. My only concern is the disturbing frequency of your episodes, Lady Clem.

LADY CLEM. I did have a very bad heartburn this morning, but I attributed that to the wretched soup.

LORD ARTHUR. Would you classify this morning's discomfort as an outright attack – an ambush, as it were – or merely a skirmish?

LADY CLEM. Arthur, you have teased me with medicines that look like sweets. And now, a foray into military metaphor. What are your motives, man?

LORD ARTHUR. To assure the well-being of a venerable relation.

LADY CLEM. I see. (*yielding*) I have often found your manners wanting, nephew – and have not hesitated to protest. But this afternoon, Arthur, I find you suitably attentive.

LORD ARTHUR. Any improvement you find in my behavior I attribute entirely to your relentless rebuke.

LADY CLEM. I share credit with Sybil, who has obviously done you a great deal of good.

LORD ARTHUR. (*wistfully*) Indeed she has. Everything I do, I do for her.

LADY CLEM. Now be gone, young man. Tonight, I am dining with some members of Parliament. If I don't get my sleep now, I shall never keep awake during dinner. Adieu, Arthur. And thank you so much for the American medicine.

LORD ARTHUR. It's the least I can do for a cherished Aunt.

LADY CLEM. I must say, your behavior today gives me hope that at long last, you have become a respectable English gentleman.

LORD ARTHUR. Thank you, madam.

LADY CLEM. With that wisdom, I may go to my grave in peace.

LORD ARTHUR. I am only too pleased to oblige. You won't forget to take the capsule, will you Lady Clem?

LADY CLEM. Of course not. But I believe my condition is improving.

LORD ARTHUR. You're feeling – better?

LADY CLEM. (*sweetly*) Yes, my dear silly boy. And I have you to thank.

LORD ARTHUR. (*anxiously*) But you're sure to have an attack by the end of the month?

LADY CLEM. I said be gone!

SCENE FIVE

Lady Windermere's Drawing Room. **LADY WIND-ERMERE**, *in mourning, and* **LORD ARTHUR**, *grinning contentedly, sit at a small table.*

LADY WINDERMERE. She dined with members of the Lower House the night before last, and from all accounts, everyone was delighted by her wit and esprit.

LORD ARTHUR. (*puzzled*) Wit and esprit? Lady Clem?

LADY WINDERMERE. Well, they are all quite deaf. She appeared to be dozing during a particularly heated discussion of gout. Then she woke with a start, emitted several odd dyspeptic sounds, and hurried home, complaining of heartburn.

LORD ARTHUR. So that's what finally did the old girl in.

LADY WINDERMERE. The next morning, she was found dead in her bed.

> **LORD ARTHUR** *leaps to his feet.*

LADY WINDERMERE. Arthur, I am aware that she was a relation, and a disagreeable one at that, but I must say I'm surprised by your high spirits.

LORD ARTHUR. Sybil was so fond of Lady Clem.

LADY WINDERMERE. Tell me, Arthur. Why did you postpone your nuptials so suddenly?

LORD ARTHUR. While certain men in my position may prefer the primrose path of dalliance to the steep heights of Duty, there is more than mere passion in my love for Sybil.

LADY WINDERMERE. Come clean, man. Why are you keeping me in the dark?

LORD ARTHUR. Lady Windermere, my esteem for you is boundless. But of late, I have been confronted by questions for which I alone must seek answers.

LADY WINDERMERE. My dear boy, sooner or later, for all of us, those same questions are asked. Men, as a rule, are asked later in life – which is why they remain close to their mothers.

LORD ARTHUR. Being motherless, I have always turned to you. But in this instance, I must act independent of your counsel.

LADY WINDERMERE. Is your simple nature equipped for such an undertaking?

LORD ARTHUR. I rely on my instincts – and those of my manservant, or course.

LADY WINDERMERE. You must rely on mine, my little cub. Exclusively.

LORD ARTHUR. That is most generous, Lady Windermere, however –

LADY WINDERMERE. And in exchange, you will tell me your secret. I am not your confidante?

LORD ARTHUR. I will tell you this, and nothing more; I adore Sybil Merton. She is a symbol of all that is good and noble.

LADY WINDERMERE. I promise not to hold that against her. Unless she insists on wearing Lady Clem's amethyst necklace, which won't be in fashion again for another eighty years.

LORD ARTHUR. You are familiar with the terms of my aunt's will?

LADY WINDERMERE. Despite many thundering threats, Lady Clem did not cut you out after all.

LORD ARTHUR. (*sincerely*) I am deeply moved. (*a beat, then*) Mr. Podgers has a great deal to answer for.

LADY WINDERMERE. Whatever do you mean, Arthur?

LORD ARTHUR. (*catching himself*) He announced her imminent demise – at a social function, no less.

LADY WINDERMERE. Not one of his most singular predictions.

LORD ARTHUR. I'm quite sure it frightened Lady Clem, and contributed, at least in part, to the heartburn which annihilated her.

LADY WINDERMERE. You have placed entirely too much faith on Podgers' prophecies. Lady Clem left that night as gay as a lark.

LORD ARTHUR. I will miss her so.

LADY WINDERMERE. Perhaps her decrepit home and furniture will keep her memory alive for you.

LORD ARTHUR. She has bequeathed all that to me?

LADY WINDERMERE. And an appalling collection of miniatures you must destroy at once.

LORD ARTHUR. I studied the Obituary column in the Times yesterday and this morning, and found nothing of Lady Clem's death, nor the terms of her will. Where did you learn this?

LADY WINDERMERE. Why should I divulge my sources to you who are so reticent with me?

LORD ARTHUR. (*a beat, then*) You may keep your secrets, Lady Windermere, just as there are secrets which shall remain locked in my heart.

LADY WINDERMERE. Do not retreat behind commonplace poetic imagery, Arthur.

LORD ARTHUR. I beg your indulgence, Lady Windermere,

for my course of action – and my metaphor.

LADY WINDERMERE. Tell me, boy. Why did you study the obituaries yesterday morning, before the body of Lady Clem had been discovered?

> **LORD ARTHUR** *looks* **LADY WINDERMERE** *in the eye.*
> **SYBIL** *enters, wearing a black silk scarf.* **LORD ARTHUR,**
> *full of glee, jumps up and hugs her.*

SYBIL. Please exhibit more appropriate restraint, sir. I am in mourning. Why did you ask to see me?

LORD ARTHUR. I have news, my love.

SYBIL. Tread lightly, Arthur. I have hardly slept since our last meeting. Mother is near collapse. It requires all my effort to mollify her.

LORD ARTHUR. I thank you for pleading my case.

SYBIL. And father is in a complete uproar – not to mention the milliners.

LORD ARTHUR. I am certain that were I to explain to them the full nature of my Task –

SYBIL. What in heavens do the milliners care about your Task?

LADY WINDERMERE. Task? What Task?

LORD ARTHUR. Your parents, Sybil. I am sure that –

SYBIL. (*interrupting*) My devotion has been lavishly tested, sir.

LORD ARTHUR. I shall never again allow anything to come between us.

SYBIL. (*cynically*) Beginning when, exactly?

LORD ARTHUR. At once. My love for you is now my single Mission. My only Duty. My –

LADY WINDERMERE. (*interrupting*) Do not speak in capital letters, boy.

SYBIL. Are you suggesting – ?

LORD ARTHUR. I have completed my Task!

SYBIL. I am overjoyed!

LADY WINDERMERE. And I am bewildered.

LORD ARTHUR. My apologies, Lady Windermere, but I felt that Sybil should be the first to know. (*to* **SYBIL**) Our wedding is on as scheduled!

SYBIL. O! Arthur!

> **SYBIL** *throws herself into* **LORD ARTHUR**'s *arms.*

LADY WINDERMERE. Let me be the first to congratulate you both. Again.

SYBIL. I must reorder the cake at once. O! the cake. If only Lady Clem had lived to see us wed. I was at her home this morning and –

LADY WINDERMERE. (*interrupting*) Whatever for?

SYBIL. I wanted to be sure that the rooms were presentable before the solicitor arrived.

LADY WINDERMERE. Very wise. Tidiness was not among her virtues. Now Sybil, you must return straight away to remove the perishables. Arthur and I have something we must discuss.

> **LADY WINDERMERE** *looks* **LORD ARTHUR** *in the eye.*

SYBIL. Look what I found at Lady Clem's! (*removes the bonbonnierre from her purse*) A little silver bonbonnierre! Isn't it quaint?

LADY WINDERMERE. Strange. There was no bonbonnierre mentioned in Lady Clem's will.

SYBIL. (*to* LORD ARTHUR) Why do you smile?

LORD ARTHUR. Curious coincidence, that's all. I gave that bonbonnierre as a gift to poor Lady Clem only the other day.

LADY WINDERMERE. What a thoughtful gesture, Arthur. I'm certain Lady Clem was delighted, and dare I say – surprised to see you at her home.

SYBIL. (*to* LORD ARTHUR) May I keep it?

LORD ARTHUR. It's what she would have wanted.

SYBIL. O! thank you, Arthur. And may I have the bonbon too?

LORD ARTHUR. (*a beat, then, gravely*) The bonbon, Sybil?

LADY WINDERMERE. She must have died suddenly, to have left even a single sweet unmolested.

LORD ARTHUR. Is there something in the box?

SYBIL removes the capsule.

SYBIL. One bonbon remains. It looks scrumptious. I shall have it at once.

She moves her hand toward her mouth. LORD ARTHUR *rushes to her and seizes the capsule from her hand, nearly knocking her down.*

SYBIL. What on earth is wrong, Arthur?

LORD ARTHUR. Sybil, I – I –

SYBIL. Good heavens, Arthur, are you ill?

LORD ARTHUR. The wedding is postponed!

SYBIL. It was already postponed!

LORD ARTHUR. Then it is – repostponed!

LORD ARTHUR *runs off.* SYBIL *chases after him.*

SYBIL. Arthur!

> **LADY WINDERMERE** *considers the bonbonnierre a moment, then rings a small bell.* **MR. PODGERS** *enters and kisses* **LADY WINDERMERE'S** *hand.*

LADY WINDERMERE. Good afternoon, Podgers.

MR. PODGERS. Good afternoon, Lady Windermere.

LADY WINDERMERE. You've missed all the excitement.

> **SYBIL** *returns. She stops when she sees* **MR. PODGERS**, *and they stare at each other a moment.*

BLACKOUT

ACT TWO

SCENE SIX

Lady Windermere's Drawing Room. **LORD ARTHUR** *paces anxiously.* **LADY WINDERMERE** *watches him closely.*

LORD ARTHUR. Lady Windermere, I am completely flummoxed! Whatever shall I do? This time, Sybil's parents are sure to call the wedding off completely.

LADY WINDERMERE. If you seek my assistance, Arthur, you must divulge at once all pertinent information related to the continual deferment and resuscitation of your nuptials.

LORD ARTHUR. I – I cannot.

LADY WINDERMERE. Tell me, boy. What did Podgers say to you at my last reception after I left the room?

LORD ARTHUR. That is confidential.

LADY WINDERMERE. He prophesied that you were to commit murder, did he not?

LORD ARTHUR. (*outraged*) I understood that my communication with Mr. Podgers was protected under cheiromantist/client privilege.

LADY WINDERMERE. Not to worry, Arthur. Podgers didn't breathe a word of it.

LORD ARTHUR. Is my behavior so transparent?

LADY WINDERMERE. It is, yes.

LORD ARTHUR. I am an incompetent murderer, Lady Windermere. I have failed miserably. The English Educational system in no way prepares a gentleman for the necessities of life.

LADY WINDERMERE. You have <u>me</u> for that.

LORD ARTHUR. I was certain poison would do the trick, given Lady Clem's fondness for ingesting medicines. But she died a natural death after all. Fate has dealt me a cruel hand.

LADY WINDERMERE. Fate is capricious. A clever woman is infallible.

LORD ARTHUR. I should have turned to you sooner, Lady Windermere.

LADY WINDERMERE. (*eagerly*) Well, if you are determined to murder someone, let's carry on!

LORD ARTHUR. What do you propose?

LADY WINDERMERE. This time, you must use something decisive.

LORD ARTHUR. Such as what?

LADY WINDERMERE. Explosives.

LORD ARTHUR. I have a natural repugnance against anything of the sort, Lady Windermere. As do all Englishmen. (*noticing Lady Windermere smiling*) Well, most.

LADY WINDERMERE. With poison, there are too many variables. Even if Lady Clem had devoured the tainted bonbon, it might have proven ineffective, given her nearly invincible constitution.

LORD ARTHUR. (*a beat, then*) You are correct, as always. Dynamite or some other form of explosive is obviously the best solution, although less – tidy than I'd hoped.

But whom shall I blow up?

LADY WINDERMERE. Sybil.

LORD ARTHUR. Lady Windermere!

LADY WINDERMERE. You are humorless, Arthur. I was in jest.

LORD ARTHUR. I'm on a Mission!

LADY WINDERMERE. We must choose someone of note. The Archdeacon of Chichester, perhaps?

LORD ARTHUR. (*mournfully*) Uncle?

LADY WINDERMERE. This sentimental posture is absurd, particularly given your recent attempt to dispatch your aunt to an early grave.

LORD ARTHUR. It was hardly an <u>early</u> grave, Lady Windermere. And I must say I am stung by the bluntness of that remark.

LADY WINDERMERE. I am frank, Arthur. Before you came under the influence of Miss Merton, you admired that quality in me.

LORD ARTHUR. I've wondered exactly what it was in <u>me</u> that <u>you</u> admired.

LADY WINDERMERE. Your potential, dear.

LORD ARTHUR. But why blow up Uncle? He is a man of great culture and learning. And a man of God.

LADY WINDERMERE. Those are among the reasons, surely. (*a beat, then*) And there is another!

LORD ARTHUR. Whatever could that be?

LADY WINDERMERE. You recall, do you not, that the Archdeacon collects timepieces?

LORD ARTHUR. Yes, cluttering up his study, as my cousin reports.

LADY WINDERMERE. His curious hobby provides an excellent opportunity for carrying out your scheme.

LORD ARTHUR. My Mission.

LADY WINDERMERE. Your murder.

LORD ARTHUR. Whatever.

LADY WINDERMERE. According to Jane, the Archdeacon is alone in his study each evening from nine till eleven. You must obtain an explosive device and have it put inside a clock.

LORD ARTHUR. What a remarkable stratagem, Lady Windermere.

LADY WINDERMERE. I am devoted to you, child.

LORD ARTHUR. Yes, however, it is the, dare I say – relish with which you have undertaken the Task that I find, dare I say – discomfiting.

LADY WINDERMERE. I have my motives, dear. Now you must send the clock as an anonymous gift. He will place it in his study, and England will have heard the last from the presiding Archdeacon of Chichester!

LORD ARTHUR. But where do I procure such a device? Shall I go to Scotland Yard?

LADY WINDERMERE. Scotland Yard never knows anything about explosions until after the fact. And fortunately for you, not much even then.

LORD ARTHUR. I admit to limited experience in this sphere, Lady Windermere.

LADY WINDERMERE. Do you remember Herr Winckelkopf? I introduced you at my last reception.

LORD ARTHUR. The unkempt solicitor?

LADY WINDERMERE. He's blown up ever so many things.

LORD ARTHUR. (*confused*) In his capacity as solicitor?

LADY WINDERMERE *sits at the table, takes a small book out of a drawer, and scribbles on a piece of paper.*

LADY WINDERMERE. Herr Winckelkopf only looks that way. He's actually a celebrated anarchist.

LORD ARTHUR. (*anxiously*) O, my.

LADY WINDERMERE. (*handing* **LORD ARTHUR** *the piece of paper*) Here is his telephone number – and his address in Soho Square. You must visit him at once.

LORD ARTHUR. Surely you don't expect me to pay a call on an anarchist at his home.

LADY WINDERMERE. I understand your concern. I'm certain his parlor is quite shabby. At my receptions, I refuse to sit anywhere near him at table.

LORD ARTHUR. Indeed. I recall that the napkin around his neck became progressively more wine-stained until he looked like a victim of the guillotine.

LADY WINDERMERE. That is a grotesque analogy, Arthur. But you must put his personal etiquette to one side.

LORD ARTHUR. It is not a question of the man's social decorum.

LADY WINDERMERE. Are you frightened of Herr Winckel-kopf?

LORD ARTHUR. (*unconvincingly*) Of course not.

LADY WINDERMERE. "Screw your courage to the sticking place," boy.

LORD ARTHUR. I hardly think Lady Macbeth should serve as inspiration here. Perhaps I could arrange to meet the man elsewhere.

LADY WINDERMERE. At your home?

LORD ARTHUR. Whatever would I ever say to Charles?

LADY WINDERMERE. Quite right. We mustn't offend the

morals of the working class.

LORD ARTHUR. (*hinting*) Unless his suspicions are even now aroused.

> **LADY WINDERMERE** *looks* **LORD ARTHUR** *in the eye, disapprovingly.*

LORD ARTHUR. I needed to tell someone, Lady Windermere.

LADY WINDERMERE. You had best accomplish this Task quickly, before half of London is complicit.

LORD ARTHUR. Might I arrange to meet Herr Winckelkopf in Hyde Park?

LADY WINDERMERE. (*impressed*) Quite good, Arthur. An anarchist will certainly go unnoticed there.

LORD ARTHUR. (*with distaste*) I seem to be spending a great deal of time al fresco since I met your Mr. Podgers.

LADY WINDERMERE. Wear a hat with a wide brim. Now, Arthur, Herr Winckelkopf is easily distracted. Be sure to explain to him that the clock must explode at 10 p.m. precisely. We wouldn't want something to go awry and blow up our dear Jane. (*enjoying herself*) Or would we?

LORD ARTHUR. I am beholden to you, Lady Windermere, for your selfless support.

LADY WINDERMERE. Not entirely selfless, Arthur. The Archdeacon shunned my receptions. This is proper punishment.

LORD ARTHUR. I am quite aware you fashion that remark to assuage any guilt I may harbor.

LADY WINDERMERE. Believe what you choose.

LORD ARTHUR. And now, to blow up Uncle.

LADY WINDERMERE. At last, my little cub, you walk among the lions!

SCENE SEVEN

Hyde Park. *An unkempt* **HERR WINCKELKOPF** *and an anxious* **LORD ARTHUR** *sit at opposite ends of a bench.*

HERR WINCKELKOPF. You require an explosive clock?

LORD ARTHUR. Unusual, I know. But I have been persuaded that it is absolutely the right thing.

HERR WINCKELKOPF. Will the explosion be domestic?

LORD ARTHUR. Yes. In the study.

HERR WINCKELKOPF. Domestic or foreign?

LORD ARTHUR. Oh, I see. Sorry. Domestic again.

HERR WINCKELKOPF. Excellent. Explosive clocks are not ideal for export. Even if they succeed in passing the Custom House, the train service is so irregular that they could go off before they reach their proper destination.

LORD ARTHUR. My wish is that the clock explodes in Chichester, Herr Winckelkopf.

HERR WINCKELKOPF. In that case, I can certainly supply an excellent piece of work, and I guarantee that you will be satisfied with the result.

LORD ARTHUR. Sir, you have set my mind at ease.

HERR WINCKELKOPF. Another question – who is the target?

LORD ARTHUR. Is it obligatory that I divulge that knowledge?

HERR WINCKELKOPF. If you intend to blow up the police, I can do nothing for you.

LORD ARTHUR. I assure you this has nothing at all to do with the police.

HERR WINCKELKOPF. I am relieved. An English detective is an anarchist's best friend.

LORD ARTHUR. I've always found the constabulary quite cordial myself.

HERR WINCKELKOPF. Are you a revolutionary?

LORD ARTHUR. O dear, no. I have no interest whatever in politics.

HERR WINCKELKOPF. The same with Lady Windermere. Social causes bore her, but she loves to hear of my explosions.

LORD ARTHUR. She admires excessive behavior for its own sake.

HERR WINCKELKOPF. The woman has opened many doors for me. I am recognized in the best circles.

LORD ARTHUR. Do you feel that it is useful nowadays for an anarchist to be accepted into London society?

HERR WINCKELKOPF. I am invited to Lady Windermere's receptions in my capacity as an artiste.

LORD ARTHUR. An artiste, you say?

HERR WINCKELKOPF. Certainment. Now to our work.

HERR WINCKELKOPF *looks about furtively, then removes a small container from his pocket and opens it.*

HERR WINCKELKOPF. Shhh.

LORD ARTHUR. That tiny box contains the explosive device?

HERR WINCKELKOPF *nods.*

LORD ARTHUR. I am quite relieved. I feared you might hand over large, unwieldy staffs I'd have to smuggle home up my sleeves.

HERR WINCKELKOPF. (*adoringly*) Mais, non! This elegant

little vessel is just the thing.

HERR WINCKELKOPF *hands* **LORD ARTHUR** *the container of dynamite.*

LORD ARTHUR. How do I get it to blow up?

HERR WINCKELKOPF. That is my concern. Let me know when you want it to explode, and I will place it inside the clock –

LORD ARTHUR. You provide the clock as well?

HERR WINCKELKOPF. (*offended*) Were you expecting a dynamite peddler?

LORD ARTHUR. Forgive me, Herr Winkelkopf, but I am unversed in the business procedures of anarchists.

HERR WINCKELKOPF. Creating an exploding device is not a business – it is an art. What type of timepiece would you like?

LORD ARTHUR. I hadn't thought about it.

HERR WINCKELKOPF. You must decide. A wall clock, a standing clock, something for the mantel – ?

LORD ARTHUR. Anything will do. (*innocently*) It won't be around for long.

HERR WINCKELKOPF. Do not speak slightingly of my work.

LORD ARTHUR. My apologies, Herr Winckelkopf.

HERR WINCKELKOPF. Would you prefer a French clock?

LORD ARTHUR. Gifts from the continent are admired, certainly.

HERR WINCKELKOPF. With ormolu figures? Or perhaps wooden carvings – ?

LORD ARTHUR. (*growing impatient*) Ormolu figures, I suppose. It's the same to me.

HERR WINCKELKOPF. Expressing what theme?

LORD ARTHUR. (*exasperated*) This is more difficult than choosing a necktie!

HERR WINCKELKOPF. Haste is ill-advised in matters of art – and explosives.

LORD ARTHUR. I am on unsure ground, Herr Winckelkopf

HERR WINCKELKOPF. Shall the theme be religious? Historical? Pastoral? Pastoral-historical?

LORD ARTHUR. Uncle delivered a sermon on License and Liberty. Does that suggest anything to you?

HERR WINCKELKOPF. Yes, it suggests that you plan to blow up your Uncle.

LORD·ARTHUR. O, my.

HERR WINCKELKOPF. And that he is of a man of the cloth.

LORD ARTHUR. Uncle is an Archdeacon who shuns society.

HERR WINCKELKOPF. I refuse to resolve a family dispute, moreover, one with Biblical implications.

LORD ARTHUR. I pursue this Task for Duty, Herr Winckelkopf. And for love.

HERR WINCKELKOPF. You intend to blow up your Uncle for love?

LORD ARTHUR. (*a beat, then*) You see, sir, I am to be wed. But there is a matter I must settle beforehand.

HERR WINCKELKOPF. I am confused.

LORD ARTHUR. I cannot untangle the web for you just now, Herr Winckelkopf, but I beg you to reconsider. (*a beat, then, desperately*) Lady Windermere speaks so highly of your accomplishments.

HERR WINCKELKOPF. Ah, Lady Windermere. She has made me a lion.

LORD ARTHUR. One of her foremost, I assure you.

HERR WINCKELKOPF. The Archdeacon's sermons consider Liberty, you say?

LORD ARTHUR. He prepared at least one on that topic, yes.

HERR WINCKELKOPF. I have just the thing! "Lady Liberty Tramples the Hydra of Despotism."

LORD ARTHUR. On a clock!?

HERR WINCKELKOPF. It's exquisitely detailed, right down to the cap on her head.

LORD ARTHUR. Brilliant. Is that everything then?

HERR WINCKELKOPF. When do you want it to explode?

LORD ARTHUR. O, yes, of course. It should blow up at ten p.m. sharp, Herr Winckelkopf. Is that clear?

HERR WINCKELKOPF. You are in sure hands.

LORD ARTHUR. (*taking out his billfold*) Now, pray let me know how much I am in your debt.

HERR WINCKELKOPF. Thank you, no. I live entirely for my art.

LORD ARTHUR. I would have thought you lived for your political ideals.

HERR WINCKELKOPF. Political ideals come and go. But an explosive device is like a moment on the stage. It exists in time – then is no more. But its memory lives forever.

LORD ARTHUR. (*impressed*) Very well put, Herr Winckelkopf, I must say.

HERR WINCKELKOPF. Would you like to know some of my friends? We're having our annual anarchist picnic this Saturday.

LORD ARTHUR. My calendar is weighed down at the

moment.

HERR WINCKELKOPF. Might I interest you in a case of nitro-glycerine bombs? I could wrap it in a medieval tapestry.

LORD ARTHUR. Thank you all the same, Herr Winckelkopf, but Uncle is the only person I need to blow up at the moment. And even there, we have a certain latitude.

HERR WINCKELKOPF. (*suspiciously*) Latitude?

LORD ARTHUR. Uncle is the preferred target, certainly – but anyone in the household would do just as well.

HERR WINCKELKOPF. That is most irregular, sir. Explosives, like art, require precision. I am afraid I must withdraw my services.

HERR WINCKELKOPF *prepares to leave.*

LORD ARTHUR. Oh, you mustn't, Herr Winckelkopf. Lady Windermere would be ever so displeased.
(*a beat, then, pointedly*) She may even be persuaded to remove you from her guest list.

LORD ARTHUR *stares* **HERR WINCKELKOPF** *in the eye.*

HERR WINCKELKOPF. A friend of Lady Windermere's is a friend of mine.

LORD ARTHUR. I must say, Herr Winckelkopf, you neither look nor behave like an anarchist.

HERR WINCKELKOPF. And you, sir, neither look nor behave like a murderer.

SCENE EIGHT

Lady Windermere's Garden. **LADY WINDERMERE** *sits on a basket chair, holding a small clock.* **JANE PERCY** *stands nearby.*

JANE. (*delighted*) It arrived early last evening in a fancy box from London, carriage paid. Papa is certain it was sent from someone inspired by his recent sermon, "Is License Liberty," because on the top of the clock – there – was a figure of a woman stepping on a reptile – here – wearing the cap of Liberty on her head. Are you familiar with the cap of Liberty, Lady Windermere?

LADY WINDERMERE. I have some knowledge of fashion during the French Revolution, yes.

JANE. I don't think it's very becoming, do you?

LADY WINDERMERE. The peasants in that period were not renowned for their millinery, Jane. Which accounts, at least in part, for their behavior. The cap <u>is</u> historical, however.

JANE. O, I suppose it's all right then. So Papa put the clock on the mantelpiece in the library, and we –

LADY WINDERMERE. (*interrupting*) In the library? I understood the Archdeacon displayed his timepieces in the study where he works.

JANE. There is no space remaining, Lady Windermere. His clocks have encroached upon the entire house. There is even one in the stables!

LADY WINDERMERE. (*disappointed*) That is obsessive, Jane, and quite possibly heretical.

JANE. We were sitting in the library when we heard a

whirring noise, and all of a sudden, a little puff of smoke came from the pedestal of the figure – there – and Lady Liberty fell off and broke her nose on the fender.

JANE *laughs uproariously.*

LADY WINDERMERE. Rein it in, Jane.

JANE. But it looked so ridiculous, Lady Windermere. Papa was alarmed at first, but after awhile, even he was amused.

LADY WINDERMERE. At what time did these events occur?

JANE. Ten o'clock in the post meridian. Afterwards, Papa examined the timepiece. He is persuaded it's a sort of alarum clock. If you put some gunpowder and a cap under the little hammer, it will go off whenever you want.

LADY WINDERMERE. (*puts the clock down quickly, and moves away*) Why have you brought it here, Jane?

JANE. Papa said it must not remain in the library, as it made noise. I suppose this type of clock is quite fashionable in London.

LADY WINDERMERE. In certain circles, yes. But my dear, if this particular timepiece is disposed to hurling mythological figures into the fireplace, surely it is faulty and we must be rid of it at once.

JANE. (*picks up the clock and clutches it tightly*) O! but I mustn't. Papa says it could do a great deal of good, as it shows that Liberty can't last and must fall down. Perhaps I might give it to Sybil as a wedding gift.

LADY WINDERMERE. Excellent idea, Jane. But there have been some developments in that area which apparently have not made their way out to Chichester. Sybil will explain.

JANE. When is she arriving?

LADY WINDERMERE. She's expected at ten (*growing suspicious*) – this morning.

JANE. And here she is now. Good morning, Sybil.

> SYBIL *enters, determined.* JANE *approaches her, still holding the clock.* LADY WINDERMERE *keeps a safe distance.*

SYBIL. Good morning, Jane. Good morning, Lady Windermere.

JANE. It is awfully kind of you to pay me a visit while I am in London, Sybil. But you look ever so fretful.

SYBIL. I have had my wedding postponed on two separate occasions, Jane.

JANE. That must be very disconcerting, Sybil.

SYBIL. Indeed, Jane, it has sent my entire family into hysteria.

JANE. Perhaps some country air would lift your spirits, dear friend.

SYBIL. That is most kind, Jane, but at the moment, I have business that requires my attention here in London.

LADY WINDERMERE. Business, Sybil? What manner of business, pray?

SYBIL. Lady Windermere, have you seen Arthur since the other day, when in your presence, he rescheduled, then repostponed our wedding?

LADY WINDERMERE. We have spoken. He fortified his resolve to accomplish his "Task."

SYBIL. Has there been any progress?

LADY WINDERMERE. None at all, I'm afraid.

JANE. I am ever so curious. What is this "Task" which Lord Arthur must accomplish?

SYBIL. That is precisely what I intend to discover, Jane. I fear that Arthur has embarked on a dangerous Mission –

JANE. A dangerous Mission! O! dear. Is my cousin involved in espionage?

SYBIL. I rather doubt it, Jane. But I have made it my Duty to discover why Arthur has chosen to pursue this mysterious Task.

LADY WINDERMERE. Those are secrets which shall remain (*cloyingly imitating* **LORD ARTHUR**) "locked away in his heart."

SYBIL. Which nonetheless, I am determined to unbolt.

LADY WINDERMERE. We must honor Arthur's request for patience, dear.

SYBIL. I will not. And I am reluctant to believe, given your nature, Lady Windermere, that you have obliged him in that regard.

JANE. This is exhilarating! Nothing of this sort ever happens in Chichester.

LADY WINDERMERE. Whatever do you mean, Sybil?

SYBIL. We were proceeding according to schedule with our wedding, until your last reception, when the cheiromantist –

JANE. The little turtle!

SYBIL. Lady Windermere, what did your palmist say to Arthur when I exited the room?

LADY WINDERMERE. I left with you, dear, as I recall.

SYBIL. Why was Mr. Podgers at your home on the day of the bonbon incident?

JANE. There has been an incident involving a bonbon!?

LADY WINDERMERE. I invited you for tea, Sybil. Is this to become an interrogation?

SYBIL. Are you or are you not providing Arthur assistance with his Task? You must tell me at once!

LADY WINDERMERE. Be civil, Sybil.

SYBIL. Where does Mr. Podgers reside?

LADY WINDERMERE. On West Moon Street. But I shall say no more until you reveal your intentions.

JANE. West Moon Street! How exotic!

From a church in the distance, a bell tolls out the time. One – Two – Three –

LADY WINDERMERE *grows anxious.*

JANE. (*to* **SYBIL**) I have just the thing to cheer you up, dear.

JANE *hands the clock to* **SYBIL**.

SYBIL. What a lovely timepiece. That's awfully sweet, Jane.

JANE. I had considered giving it to you as a wedding gift, but you may keep it even if the wedding is off.

SYBIL. How kind.

*The church bells ring louder now – Six – Seven – Eight – **LADY WINDERMERE** hesitates, then charges at **SYBIL** – Nine –. She grabs the clock and flings it into the garden (offstage). A loud explosion, and a few leaves tumble onto the stage. The three women stand frozen a few moments, then:*

LADY WINDERMERE. I'll ring for tea.

SCENE NINE

Lord Arthur's Rooms. **LORD ARTHUR** *paces about, completely unstrung, as* **CHARLES** *watches anxiously.*

LORD ARTHUR. Twice now, inadvertently, I have almost done away with the woman I love!

CHARLES. Twice, sir?

LORD ARTHUR. Sybil was nearly detonated, Charles. By an exploding clock!

CHARLES. This suggests Lady Windermere's counsel.

LORD ARTHUR. She pressured me, Charles, and I succumbed.

CHARLES. But the clock proved defective?

LORD ARTHUR. It made a minor puff at ten in the evening, then a major eruption at ten in the morning – only a moment after it was wrenched from my dear Sybil's hands.

CHARLES. I am loathe to inquire as to whom Lady Windermere had hoped to demolish.

LORD ARTHUR. The Archdeacon of Chichester, Charles. (**CHARLES** *is extremely dismayed*) He collects clocks. It seemed a good idea at the time.

CHARLES. I understood that you had placed this matter entirely in my hands.

LORD ARTHUR. My mistake, Charles. I should never rely on anyone I meet at Lady Windermere's receptions.

CHARLES. She is a hazardous influence, and I beg you to keep your distance.

LORD ARTHUR. Yesterday, Charles, I attempted to coerce a celebrated anarchist. And I was censured.

CHARLES. Censured by an anarchist?

LORD ARTHUR. Yes, Charles. I am ashamed to admit that my actions toward him were shoddy, and deserving of his reproach.

CHARLES. That woman has led you down dangerous paths, sir.

LORD ARTHUR. You don't know the half. When Lady Windermere told me what had nearly happened to Sybil, I ran from her house and wandered along the Thames Embankment. It was there that I resolved to accomplish my Mission alone, without poisons or exploding clocks to do my work for me. Are you following my meaning, Charles?

CHARLES. (*with growing concern*) I am, sir.

LORD ARTHUR. So I set about looking for a victim.

CHARLES. Dangerous paths indeed.

LORD ARTHUR. But it was not as easy as I thought. I tried to push a clergyman under the wheels of an omnibus, but he jumped back suddenly, stepped on my feet and ran off without so much as an apology. I shoved a woman into the canal, but she was saved by a passerby, and I had to recompense the both of them. I overturned a perambulator containing a young child. He was highly entertained, and insisted I do it again.

CHARLES. A wicked woman's parlor game has put the entire citizenry of London at risk.

LORD ARTHUR. The time has come to break off the marriage for good. Sybil will grieve, it's true, but suffering could never really tarnish a nature as noble as hers.

CHARLES. I implore you – cease with this foolish Task, and proceed with the marriage.

LORD ARTHUR. You don't understand. How could you? You see, Charles, a gentleman must do his Duty.

CHARLES. You are placing yourself in grave danger, my lord.

LORD ARTHUR. But without Sybil, I have nothing to live for. Life no longer holds pleasure, and death has no terror.

CHARLES. (*a beat, then*) What is your inference, sir?

LORD ARTHUR. If Destiny has death in store for me, then die I must.

CHARLES. (*urgently*) I shall get your waistcoat. And your gloves.

LORD ARTHUR. Whatever for?

CHARLES. The time has come to take a journey. And at once.

LORD ARTHUR. To where?

CHARLES. West Moon Street.

LORD ARTHUR. West Moon Street? Whatever for?

SCENE TEN

Lady Windermere's Drawing Room. A small table with chairs and a few larger chairs. Offstage, the sound of chatter from guests in other rooms. **LADY WINDERMERE** *and* **SYBIL** *enter.*

SYBIL. I haven't seen so many extravagantly dressed people in a long while, Lady Windermere.

LADY WINDERMERE. That is most kind. And no doubt, true.

SYBIL. I hope you don't mind that I am attending your reception without invitation.

LADY WINDERMERE. Not at all, dear. The mysterious circumstances surrounding your perpetually postponed nuptials have made you a marginally more intriguing figure.

SYBIL. If only Lady Clem were here with us!

LADY WINDERMERE. That might startle the guests.

SYBIL. It is in her memory that I wear this amethyst necklace.

LADY WINDERMERE. I must be candid, dear. As a display of sentimentality, it is excusable. As a display of fashion, it is unconscionable.

SYBIL. In certain circumstances, one must disregard fashion.

LADY WINDERMERE. That is the only truly shocking statement I have ever heard you utter.

JANE barges in. She is wearing a preposterous dress covered with bows, and large petticoats beneath.

JANE. Lady Windermere, your reception is ever so invigorating!

SYBIL. Jane, I must be candid. I have never seen so many bows on one dress in my life.

LADY WINDERMERE. Nor undergarments so voluminous.

SYBIL. However are you able to maneuver among the crowd?

JANE. (*proudly*) They made way when they saw me approach.

LADY WINDERMERE. Please notify me in advance if you are to wear something of such magnitude to my next reception, as I shall invite fewer guests.

JANE. When I dropped a tray of crudités and bent over to pick it up, at once, all of the bishops rushed to assist me.

SYBIL. I am certain that they never imagined such a sight – even in their celestial visions.

JANE. Where is Lord Arthur? I must learn if there have been any developments with his secret Mission.

LADY WINDERMERE. Sybil and I were wondering the same thing. (*to* **SYBIL**) Isn't that why you came, dear?

JANE. I must say I am disappointed that Mr. Podgers will not be in attendance this evening, Lady Windermere. But I am eager to hear your views on his murder.

LADY WINDERMERE and **SYBIL** *freeze, then look each other in the eye.*

LADY WINDERMERE. What – what's this?

JANE. It appears that yesterday noon, the body of Mr. Podgers was found in his West Moon Street residence.

SYBIL. (*simply*) I'm certain that considerable anguish will be felt in cheiromantic circles.

LORD ARTHUR *enters, wearing gloves.*

LORD ARTHUR. Good evening, Sybil.

SYBIL. Good evening, Arthur.

LORD ARTHUR. Lady Winderemere. Cousin.

LADY WINDERMERE. Mr. Podgers is murdered, Arthur – have you heard?

LORD ARTHUR. You don't say.

SYBIL. Where did you learn this, Jane?

JANE. A group of gentlemen on the terrace, having read the obituary column in the Times, are discussing the particulars.

SYBIL. Are you certain the Times stated that Podgers was, in fact, murdered?

JANE. I am assured, dear friend.

LORD ARTHUR. On what did they base this – hypothesis?

JANE. There were hand marks around his neck, but no fingerprints.

SYBIL. Apparently the murderer wore gloves to conceal identification.

LADY WINDERMERE. That narrows the suspects down to someone in society. The lower order is loathe to – accessorize.

SYBIL. There is no such word, Lady Windermere

LADY WINDERMERE. (*pleased with herself*) There is now. I christen it.

JANE. Why on earth anyone would want to murder a little noodle like Mr. Podgers?

SYBIL. A vast array of reasons, Jane.

LORD ARTHUR. Indeed, it's exactly what he deserved.

LADY WINDERMERE. Arthur, why do you harbor such ill will toward poor Mr. Podgers? Do you still believe the man could actually tell palms?

LORD ARTHUR. Shouldn't I?

LADY WINDERMERE. Foolish boy. I would tell Podgers everything I knew about my guests. Then he would pretend to read this information in their hands.

SYBIL. As I suspected.

> **LORD ARTHUR** *turns away.*

LADY WINDERMERE. This was amusing for a time.

SYBIL. (*to* **LORD ARTHUR**, *lightly*) Say something, darling.

LORD ARTHUR. How could you perpetrate such a fraud, Lady Windermere?

LADY WINDERMERE. Be kind, dear.

LORD ARTHUR. Is this what your guests can expect – moreover, what <u>I</u> can expect? To attend your receptions and be set upon by that – that –

JANE. (*helpfully*) Minimus?

LORD ARTHUR. You deliberately misled me, Lady Windermere.

LADY WINDERMERE. I endeavored to explain that the man was merely an entertainer, but you were on and on about your "Duty."

SYBIL. Arthur, what did Podgers say to you that night when we left the room?

LORD ARTHUR. I – I can't.

LADY WINDERMERE. What are you afraid of, dear? If Sybil is to be your wife, you mustn't have any secrets. Isn't that your policy, Sybil?

SYBIL. It is indeed. Arthur, did Podgers say that you were to commit a murder?

LORD ARTHUR. (*startled*) How do you know?

SYBIL. I deduced it.

LADY WINDERMERE. Very cunning, Sybil.

JANE. (*impressed*) O! my. So <u>you</u> are the murderer, cousin. How utterly surprising!

LADY WINDERMERE. Indeed, Jane. Who would deem Arthur qualified to accomplish such a feat without assistance?

SYBIL. And you, Lady Windermere, encouraged the dreadful little man to goad Arthur into homicide.

LADY WINDERMERE. In fact, I was quite eager for Podgers to read <u>your</u> hand, as you recall.

SYBIL. Whatever for?

LADY WINDERMERE. (*gloatingly*) Must I divulge all of my secrets?

SYBIL. What information about me could you possibly provide? I am morally unassailable.

LADY WINDERMERE. That's always been your deficiency, Sybil. In fact, I was forced to <u>invent</u> something. Characteristically, however, you declined to behave as a proper guest and sit for your reading.

SYBIL. And inciting Arthur to murder was your alternate strategy?

LADY WINDERMERE. Actually, no. When Arthur volunteered, Podgers knew he had to improvise. I must say, the man exceeded my expectations. Murder was just the thing! But it was entirely Podgers' idea – and if the Times is to be believed, his undoing. It was never part of my plan.

LORD ARTHUR. What <u>was</u> your plan, exactly?

LADY WINDERMERE. Once and for all, to put an end to your unfortunate interest in such an ordinary girl.

JANE. I must confess, Sybil. Your frocks <u>are</u> quite plain. I've always meant to discuss this with you.

LORD ARTHUR. Lady Windermere, you have betrayed me.

LADY WINDERMERE. It was for your own good, Arthur.

SYBIL. You were quite certain that if Arthur took someone's life, it would temper my love for him?

LADY WINDERMERE. I am familiar with your type, Sybil; "Averse to scandal."

SYBIL. And that I would cancel the wedding?

LADY WINDERMERE. There, my secret is out.

LORD ARTHUR. I see now why you were so eager to assist me. Does murder mean nothing to you, Lady Windermere?

SYBIL. It means something to <u>me</u>, dear. (**LORD ARTHUR** *turns away.* **LADY WINDERMERE** *smiles. A beat, then*) How many women can say that their husband would kill for them?

LADY WINDERMERE. (*a beat, then, horrified*) What are you saying, Sybil?

SYBIL. So sorry to disappoint you, dear. But the successful completion of Arthur's Task has only increased my admiration for him.

LORD ARTHUR. (*overjoyed*) My dear one!

SYBIL. Everything you did, my love, you did for me.

> **LORD ARTHUR** *and* **SYBIL** *embrace.*

LADY WINDERMERE. (*bitterly disappointed*) Of that – lamentably – there has never been a doubt.

JANE. I must say, at this moment, I am fully confused. Is the wedding on or off?

LORD ARTHUR. The wedding is on!

SYBIL. All is restored, Arthur – just as you promised.

LORD ARTHUR. Which is precisely what is required in comedy.

LADY WINDERMERE. And farce.

JANE. O! my. I must find something astonishing to wear.

SYBIL. I doubt that you can surpass tonight's ensemble.

JANE. I promise one and all, in the presence of God, I shall endeavor to do just that!

> JANE *runs off.*

SYBIL. (*to* LORD ARTHUR) Come along, dear. We must resume our preparations. I shall reorder the cake. O! the cake. If only Lady Clem had lived to see our wedding day!

LORD ARTHUR. The last time I saw my ancient aunt, she assured me that I had become a perfect English gentleman.

LADY WINDERMERE. Are you suggesting that an Englishman's Duty is to murder irritable relations?

LORD ARTHUR. Well, at that precise moment, she had me entirely wrong. But I'm sure that Lady Clem would be quite proud of me now. I have found my Duty at last. And it is not murder. It is a lifelong devotion to the woman I love! What more could I ask?

LADY WINDERMERE. Much more, Arthur. Much more.

LORD ARTHUR. I have everything I desire, Lady Windermere. Isn't that what you've always wanted for me?

LADY WINDERMERE. I'm growing increasingly weary, Arthur. I believe this reception will be my last.

LORD ARTHUR. London society will never be the same. It is the end of an era.

SYBIL. And not a moment too soon. Arthur, perhaps we should divest ourselves of Lady Clem's home and relocate to Chichester.

LADY WINDERMERE. Relocate? There is no such word.

SYBIL. There is now.

LORD ARTHUR. Goodnight Lady Windermere.

> **SYBIL** *takes* **LORD ARTHUR** *by the arm.* **LADY WINDERMERE** *stands.*

LADY WINDERMERE. Please be so kind as to stay for dinner. My new pet is here tonight, Arthur – a telepathist.

LORD ARTHUR. What's a telepathist, Lady Windermere?

SYBIL. Come along, Arthur!

LADY WINDERMERE. He knows what we're all thinking. He can see into our minds.

SYBIL. Without any assistance from you?

LADY WINDERMERE. (*to* **LORD ARTHUR**, *using all her charm*) I beg you to reconsider, dear.

> **LORD ARTHUR** *stands directly between* **SYBIL** *and* **LADY WINDERMERE**. *Both women await his decision anxiously.*

LORD ARTHUR. I'm afraid I would bore a telepathist silly, Lady Windermere. Apart from thoughts of Sybil, there is nothing whatever going on in <u>my</u> mind.

> **SYBIL** *takes* **LORD ARTHUR** *by the hand, and they head off.* **LADY WINDERMERE** *stares out.*

THE END

FURNITURE PLOT

Scene 1
A small table, with two chairs (for palm readings)
Two "more comfortable" chairs
A cocktail cart

Scene 2
A writing table
A chair

Scene 3
A park bench

Scene 4
A divan

Scene 5
Same as Scene 1

Scene 6
Same as Scene 1

Scene 7
Same as Scene 3

Scene 8
Two "basket" chairs, i.e., garden or outdoor furniture

Scene 9
Same as Scene 2

Scene 10
Same as Scene 1

PROPERTY PLOT

Scene 1
Lady Clem's fan
Lady Clem's medicines
Wine glasses
Cocktail glasses
Water pitcher
Various alcohol bottles
Mr. Podgers' business card
Card holder
Mr. Podgers' handkercheif

Scene 2
Framed photo of Sybil
Writing tablet
Pen
Checkbook
Mr. Podgers' card (same as Scene 1)

Scene 3
Bouquet of Narcissi

Scene 4
Books
Medicines
Lady Clem's fan
Gelatin capsule (bonbon)
Bonbonnierre (silver box, elaborate almost like jewelry)

Scene 5
Bonbonnierre (same as Scene 4)
A hand bell

Scene 6
Stationary
Pen

Scene 7
Small pocket size container (for the explosives)

Scene 8
Clock (as described in Scene 7)
Amethyst necklace (costume)

Scene 9
Same as Scene 2

Scene 10
Same cocktail cart as Scene 1

HAZELWOOD JR. HIGH

Rob Urbinati

Drama / 6f

At first, Hazelwood Jr. High is like any other middle school – cliques and crushes, dances and detention. But when a new girl unwittingly steps into a "love triangle," a revenge plot is hatched, and events spin out of control, escalating into a shocking and unimaginable climax. Based on a true story.

"Mr. Urbinati's script is based on court testimony and psychological and police reports. Even in the era of Jeffrey Dahlmer and Susan Smith, the story holds its own grotesquerie; you can see why Mr. Urbinati was hooked by it. It takes the absolutely ordinary subject of teenage rivalry and revenge pranks, gives it an exotic lesbian twist and then pushes it to the outer limits of sociopathic behavior. Mr. Elliott, Mr. Urbinati and the cast do nicely in conveying the solemn earnestness of young love and social warfare."
– Ben Brantley, *The New York Times*

"*Hazelwood Jr. High* is a blistering piece of drama that's conceived and presented in cinematic terms. Its multiple scenes and locations flow into each other without a break, building a considerable I can't believe I'm watching this steam as Urbinati's story veers from puppydog lesbian romance toward brutal slaughter. The horror of it all is seriocomically underscored by the typical banalities of teen existence while songs by Mariah Carey and 1990's girl groups pulse through the air. If you go, better hang on tight – it's a wicked midnight ride with the rising generation, and definitely not a show for the squeamish."
- Michael Sommers, *New Jersey Star Ledger*

SAMUELFRENCH.COM

THE SCENE
Theresa Rebeck

Little Theatre / Drama / 2m, 2f / Interior Unit Set
A young social climber leads an actor into an extra-marital affair, from which he then creates a full-on downward spiral into alcoholism and bummery. His wife runs off with his best friend, his girlfriend leaves, and he's left with… nothing.

"Ms. Rebeck's dark-hued morality tale contains enough fresh insights into the cultural landscape to freshen what is essentially a classic boy-meets-bad-girl story."
- *New York Times*

"Rebeck's wickedly scathing observations about the sort of self-obsessed New Yorkers who pursue their own interests at the cost of their morality and loyalty."
- *New York Post*

"The Scene is utterly delightful in its comedic performances, and its slowly unraveling plot is thought-provoking and gut-wrenching."
- *Show Business Weekly*

THREE MUSKETEERS
Ken Ludwig

All Groups / Adventure / 8m, 4f (doubling) / Unit sets
This adaptation is based on the timeless swashbuckler by Alexandre Dumas, a tale of heroism, treachery, close escapes and above all, honor. The story, set in 1625, begins with d'Artagnan who sets off for Paris in search of adventure. Along with d'Artagnan goes Sabine, his sister, the quintessential tomboy. Sent with d'Artagnan to attend a convent school in Paris, she poses as a young man – d'Artagnan's servant – and quickly becomes entangled in her brother's adventures. Soon after reaching Paris, d'Artagnan encounters the greatest heroes of the day, Athos, Porthos and Aramis, the famous musketeers; d'Artagnan joins forces with his heroes to defend the honor of the Queen of France. In so doing, he finds himself in opposition to the most dangerous man in Europe, Cardinal Richelieu. Even more deadly is the infamous Countess de Winter, known as Milady, who will stop at nothing to revenge herself on d'Artagnan – and Sabine – for their meddlesome behavior. Little does Milady know that the young girl she scorns, Sabine, will ultimately save the day.

THE MUSICAL OF MUSICALS (THE MUSICAL!)
Music by Eric Rockwell
Lyrics by Joanne Bogart
Book by Eric Rockwell and Joanne Bogart

2m, 2f / Musical / Unit Set
The Musical of Musicals (The Musical!) is a musical about musicals! In this hilarious satire of musical theatre, one story becomes five delightful musicals, each written in the distinctive style of a different master of the form, from Rodgers and Hammerstein to Stephen Sondheim. The basic plot: June is an ingenue who can't pay the rent and is threatened by her evil landlord. Will the handsome leading man come to the rescue? The variations are: a Rodgers & Hammerstein version, set in Kansas in August, complete with a dream ballet; a Sondheim version, featuring the landlord as a tortured artistic genius who slashes the throats of his tenants in revenge for not appreciating his work; a Jerry Herman version, as a splashy star vehicle; an Andrew Lloyd Webber version, a rock musical with themes borrowed from Puccini; and a Kander & Ebb version, set in a speakeasy in Chicago. This comic valentine to musical theatre was the longest running show in the York Theatre Company's 35-year history before moving to Off-Broadway.

"Witty! Refreshing! Juicily! Merciless!"
- Michael Feingold, *Village Voice*

"A GIFT FROM THE MUSICAL THEATRE GODS!"
– *TalkinBroadway.com*

"Real Wit, Real Charm! Two Smart Writers and Four Winning Performers! You get the picture, it's GREAT FUN!"
- *The New York Times*

"Funny, charming and refreshing!
It hits its targets with sophisticated affection!"
- *New York Magazine*

SAMUELFRENCH.COM

THE OFFICE PLAYS
Two full length plays by Adam Bock

THE RECEPTIONIST
Comedy / 2m., 2f. Interior

At the start of a typical day in the Northeast Office, Beverly deals effortlessly with ringing phones and her colleague's romantic troubles. But the appearance of a charming rep from the Central Office disrupts the friendly routine. And as the true nature of the company's business becomes apparent, The Receptionist raises disquieting, provocative questions about the consequences of complicity with evil.

"...Mr. Bock's poisoned Post-it note of a play."
- New York Times

"Bock's intense initial focus on the routine goes to the heart of *The Receptionist's* pointed, painfully timely allegory... elliptical, provocative play..."
- Time Out New York

THE THUGS
Comedy / 2m, 6f / Interior

The Obie Award winning dark comedy about work, thunder and the mysterious things that are happening on the 9th floor of a big law firm. When a group of temps try to discover the secrets that lurk in the hidden crevices of their workplace, they realize they would rather believe in gossip and rumors than face dangerous realities.

"Bock starts you off giggling, but leaves you with a chill."
- Time Out New York

"... a delightfully paranoid little nightmare that is both more chillingly realistic and pointedly absurd than anything John Grisham ever dreamed up."
- New York Times

Breinigsville, PA USA
05 January 2011
252706BV00004B/13/P